WHAT GRANDMAS DO BEST

BY **Laura Numeroff**

ILLUSTRATED BY **Lynn Munsinger**

In loving memory of my grandparents
—L.N.

In memory of my beloved grandmother
Dorothy Chancellor Currey
—L.M.

WHAT GRANDMAS DO BEST

BY **Laura Numeroff**

ILLUSTRATED BY **Lynn Munsinger**

SCHOLASTIC INC.
New York Toronto London Auckland Sydney
Mexico City New Delhi Hong Kong Buenos Aires

Grandmas can play hide-and-seek,

make you a hat,

and take you for a walk.

Grandmas can paint with you,

show you their photographs,

and teach you how to dance.

Grandmas can take you on a picnic,

show you some magic tricks,

and help you fly a kite.

Grandmas can take you to the beach,

help you build a sand castle,

and take a nap with you.

Grandmas can play games with you,

give you a bath,

and sing you a lullaby.

But best of all,
Grandmas can give you
lots and lots of love.

But best of all,
Grandpas can give you
lots and lots of love.

and sing you a lullaby.

give you a bath,

Grandpas can play games with you,

and take a nap with you.

help you build a sand castle,

Grandpas can take you to the beach,

and help you fly a kite.

show you some magic tricks,

Grandpas can take you on a picnic,

and teach you how to dance.

show you their photographs,

Grandpas can paint with you,

and take you for a walk.

make you a hat,

Grandpas can play hide-and-seek,

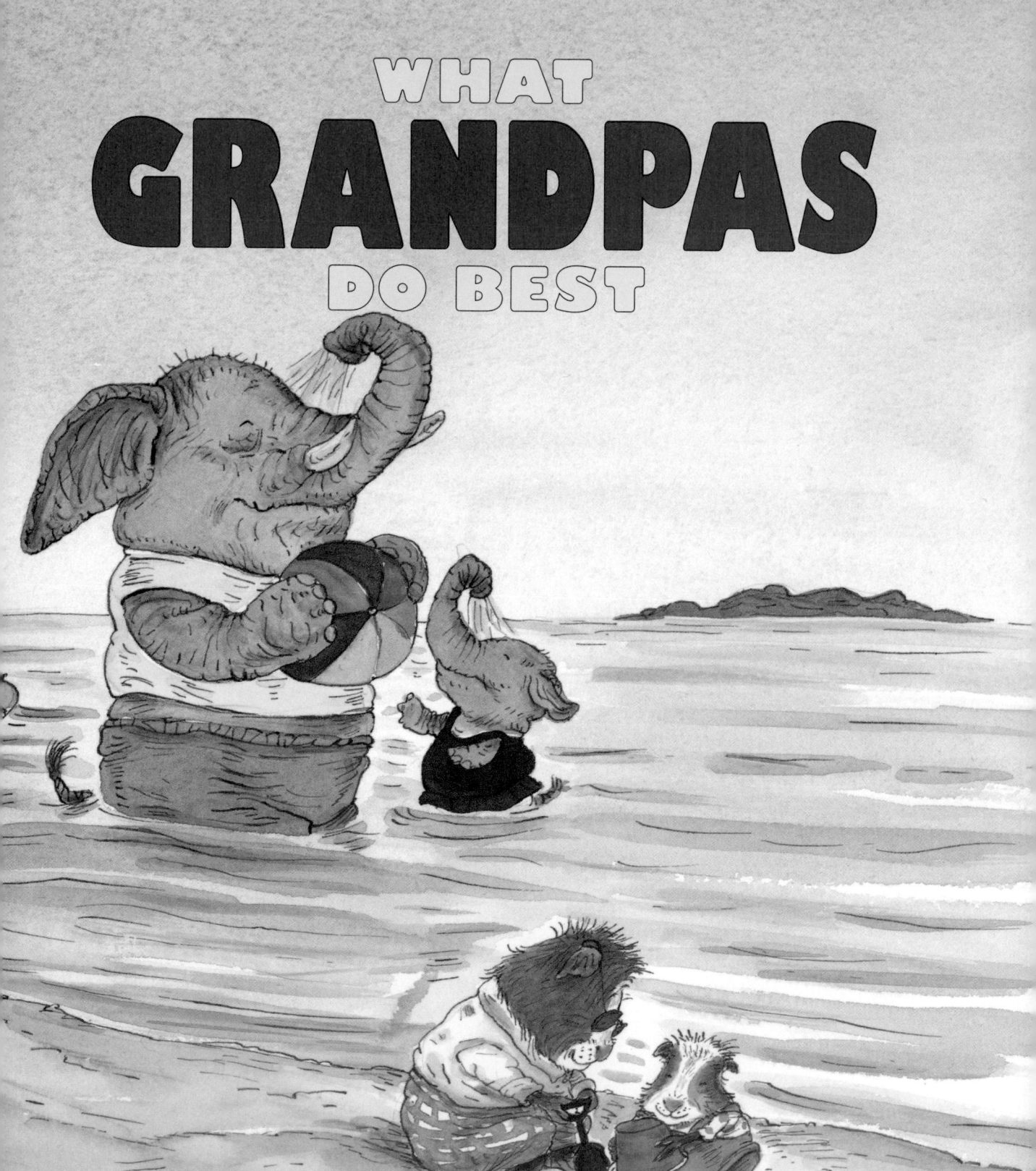

WHAT
GRANDPAS
DO BEST

Also by Laura Numeroff/Lynn Munsinger
WHAT MOMMIES DO BEST/WHAT DADDIES DO BEST